SLEEP

WRITTEN BY

Charles Anthony Silvestri

ILLUSTRATED BY

Anne Horjus

ACROTERION BOOKS 2013

For Thomas, who inspired it then;
For Julie, who gives it meaning now.
C. A. S.

For DeDe, who is always standing behind my chair
and looking over my shoulder.
A. H.

www.acroterionbooks.com

The text in this book is set in Times New Roman.
The illustrations are rendered in graphite pencils and airbrush.

Library of Congress Cataloging-in-Publication Data

Silvestri, Charles Anthony
Sleep / written by Charles Anthony Silvestri ; illustrated by Anne Horjus.
p. cm.
Summary: A young boy finds comfort after his loss, while falling asleep.
EAN/ISBN-13: 978-1480-35402-9
[1. Sleep-Poetry. 2. American Poetry]
PZ7.S588454 Sl 2013
811'.6-dcc

Manufactured in the United States of America
1 3 5 7 9 10 8 6 4 2

EXCLUSIVELY DISTRIBUTED BY

HAL•LEONARD®
CORPORATION
7777 W. BLUEMOUND RD. P.O. BOX 13819 MILWAUKEE, WI 53213

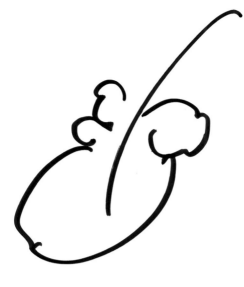

SLEEP

The evening hangs
beneath the moon,

A silver thread
on darkened dune.

With closing eyes
and resting head
I know that sleep
is coming soon.

Upon my pillow,
safe in bed,

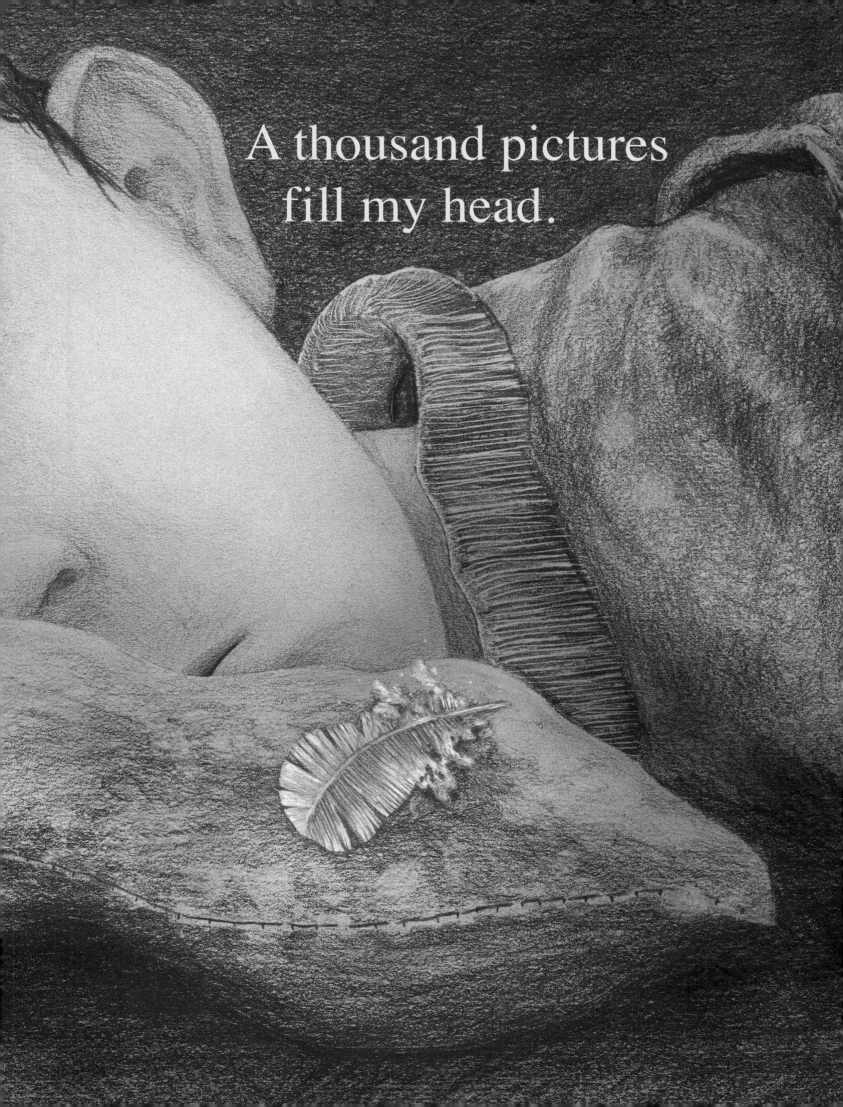

A thousand pictures
fill my head.

I cannot sleep,
my mind's a-flight;

And yet my limbs
seem made of lead.

If there are noises
in the night,

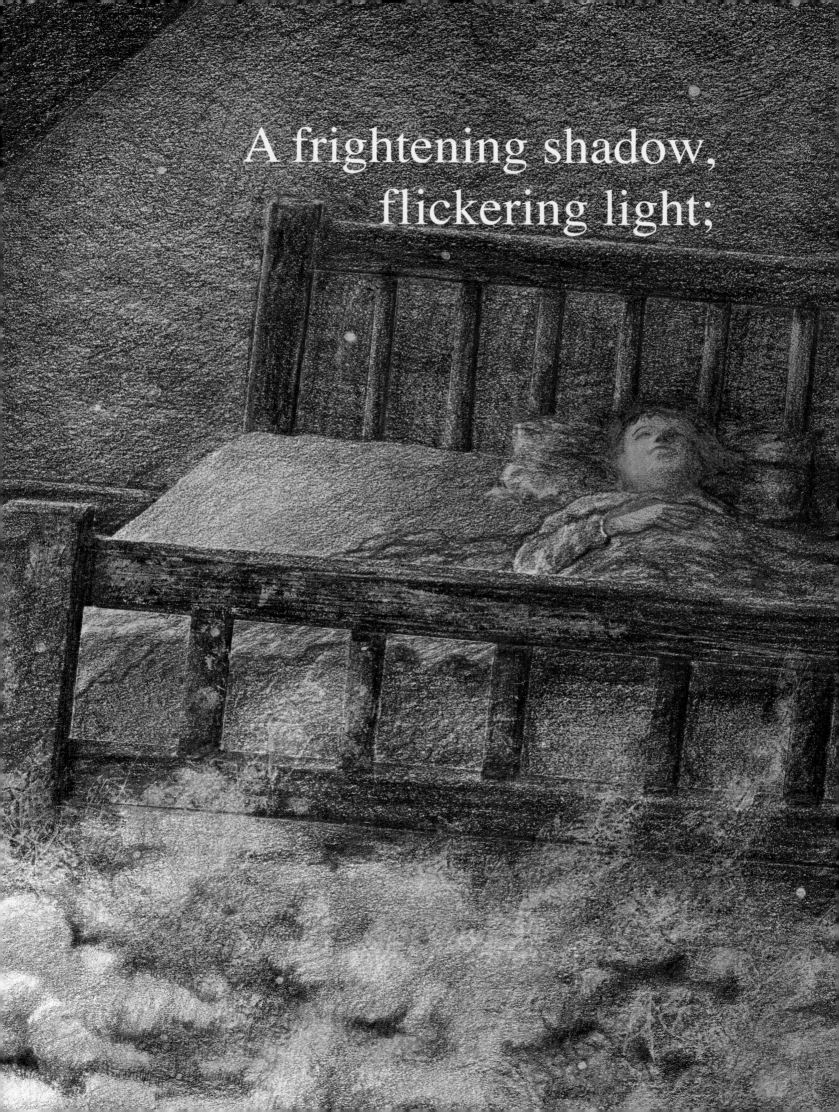

Then I surrender unto sleep,

Where clouds of dream
give second sight,

What dreams may come,
both dark and deep,

Of flying wings

and soaring leap

As I surrender
unto sleep,

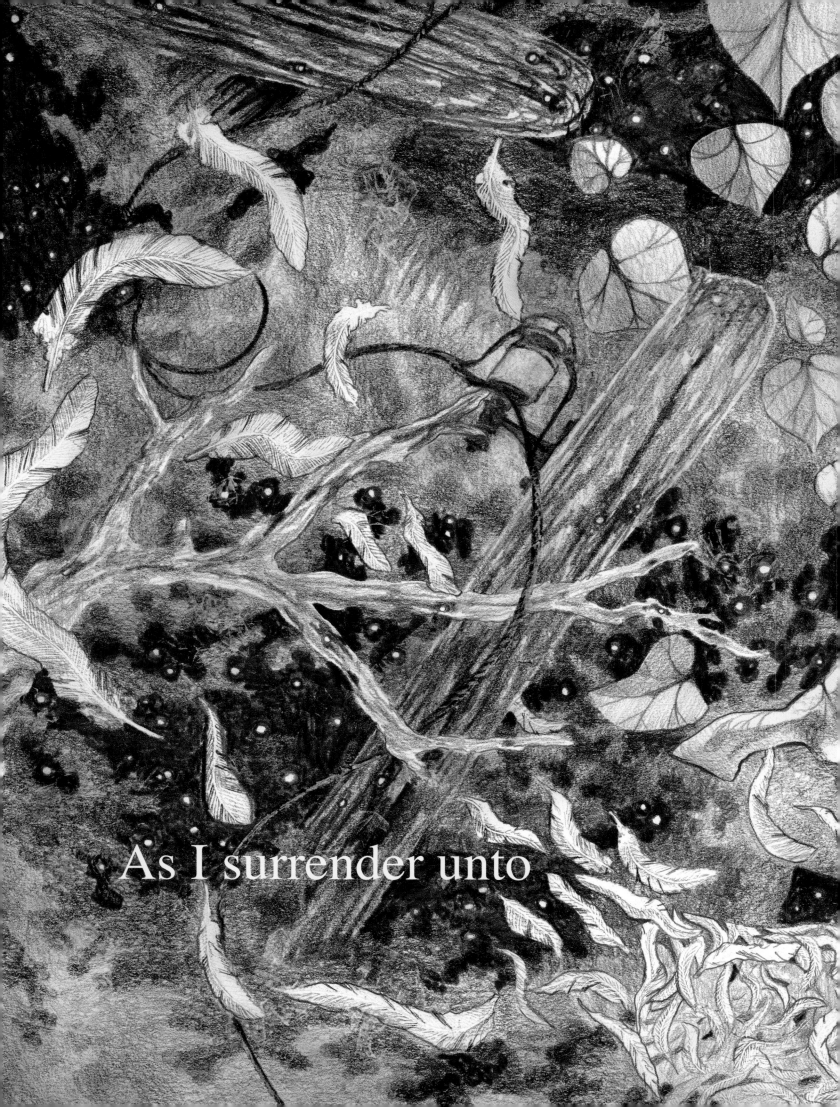

As I surrender unto

sleep.

Thank you to our generous supporters! Without you this publication would not have been possible. Here is a list of our Kickstarters in alphabetical order.

Neil L Aaronson   Francena D Abendroth   Melissa Adams   The Aldridge Family   Jennifer R Allen   Meg & Scott All

Cheryl Lynn Anderson   Matt & Aleasha Anderson   Anelamalulani   Anonymous   Rhona-Mae Arca & Musespeak Stud

Jared Aswegan   L M Attea   Alexander L Bak   Shana C Baker   Baraboo Philosophical Society   Anna M Barker   Lizabeth Barnett   Steve Bartl

Steve Beckett   Christina Beam   Sleepy Becky   Kailey Bennett   Adam Bideau   Jimmie & Candance Bise   Patricia Bla

Adam Blackman   Ryan Michael Bogner   Tod & Beth Bolsinger   Dash Frank Boucher   Sherry Bowden   Madyson Adair Boy

Marian M Boykin   Xa Braga   Ellen Braun   Donald Brinegar   Christopher Stewart Brown   Holly Christine Brov

David & Jessica Bryan   Jerry & Pat Bullard   Claire Burrell-McDonald   Jack & Ann Burton   Diane Campbell   Alexandra J Carl

Ethan Carlson   Kimberly Carlson   Jennifer Carnevale   Jason P, Amy B, & Madeleine P Caron   Katherine Ch

Lawrence "The Dreamer" Chen   Jennifer Christensen   Carissa Christner   Aaron P Churchill   Licia K Clark   Natalie Gunn Coffm

Evan Cohen   The Coleman Family   Alexis Colpoys   John Conahan   Sharon R Conrad   Mallory C Cook   Natalie Cool   Max Cord

Kim Morse Cordova   Jonathan Christian Cosas   David Cousins   Monica Cox   Mary Craven   John R Crawley   Marie Cummin

Jordan Spencer Cunningham, Esquire   Alex Cutler   Julia Dempsey Daily   Jason P Daly   Sean Davis   Tresa Gillman Dav

Martha C Dawson   Faith DeBow   Carley DeFranco   Pauline de Heer   Kirsten Dean   Gabriella Rose Der

John & Marilyn Devorick   Sue Dietsch   Gary Doering   Robert Doole   Case & Annemarie Dorresteyn   Mara Doughty   Liz Dov

June Dowad   Thadeus Dowad   Thomas, Bridget & Elora Doxtater   Gretchen Dresen   Judith Drotar   David & Julie Dunlap   Brendan Dun

Becky Ziegel Duranceau   Susan Mills Durham   Derek J Duzan   Juanita Edington   David M Eilers   My Beloved Eleanor   Judith M Ellingto

Marco Antonio Estrada   Ted Evans   Matthew Faerber   Neal McQueen Farley   Eric M Ferring   Austin Fields   Barbara Fi

Thomas Flock   The Flying Circus   Carolyn Porter Flynn   Lisa (Zilpha) Banlaki Frank   Raymond Frankulin   Helene Silver Fre

Adam B Friedman   Anita Dann Friedman   Spike Friedman   Los Frijoles   Miriam Rheingold Fuller   Angelica Fule

Simon, Hannah & Ella Funnell   Robert Garcia   Angela & Andrew Gardner   Dawn R Garski   Dave & Carrie Gaste

Sally Goodwin   Miguel Ángel Gonzáles-Abellás   Nina Anne M Greeley   James R Green   Robert Greenham   Melissa Grace Grego

Gail & Dan Greve   Nathaniel Grill   Jerome Grisanti   Leslie Griswold   Justin Gronholz   Margaret Grove   Meredith Guzm

Jennifer Hagar   Erik, Michelle & Dorian Hagen   Colette Halliday   Jason & Stacie Hanson   Gil & Hilda Hantzsch   Haley Hanz

Emily Faye Hare   Lilith Hart   Stephanie Heinrich   Craig Herrington   Gloria Heyde   Anita Hibbard   Sarah Higley   Donna Hill   David Hin

Mark Hirschman   Kathy Hoelter   Rebecca Hoenig   Monica Holden   Michael Allen Hollinger   Sarah Hollyman   Tom & Sue Holm

Steven C Holovach   Lorrie Holt   Annemariske Horjus   John & Meredith Houge   Kathy Houzner   Jeff & Kristen Huenemann   Ashley Huffo

Rebecca Hunt   Jesse Hunter   Samuel Hunter   Brigitta Camille Hutchins   Mark & Lisa Ingles   Laura Inman   Katarzyna Iskrz

Tom & Carol Lee Iverson   Rich Jacobson   Laura Jaget   Amy Myers Jensen   Joanna   Sarah Joblin   Dallas N Johnson   Deanna M Johnso

Erin Johnson   Penny Johnson   Ben Jones   Joshua Jordan   John A Jorgensen & Olga Pomolova   Ben Joseph   Megan Kalman   Yasmin Karim

Sandra E Kece   Julie Keller   Andrea Rose Kiddoo   Tori Kieschnick   Austin Kiley   James Hyongsup Kim   Stuart Kime   The Kinzer Fami

Lory Y Kitamura-Tintor   Kathrin Klaar   Sue Klaus   Genevieve Klein   Leah Klein   Margaret M Klein   Adam G Kloo

Hannah Elaine Knott   Rachel Knott   Catherine S Koch   Mike & Karin Jo Kohlman   Michael Kregor   The Krszjzaniek Fami

Annika Kukk   Candice Kuzov   Danielle LaDue   Annemie Lamon   Lauren Lamonsoff   Amanda Lang & Matthew Schlun

Jamie "Big Dog" Lang   Jeff Lang   Tina Lang   Ruth B LeBlanc   Marie Lemenu   Vickie Lepore   J D Lewis   Nikki Lewis

Claire Long   Jason, Amy, Charlotte & Violet Longtin   The Lorimer Family   Joseph H Loso   Alison Love   Lauren Love